Postman Pat
and the Mystery Thief

Story by John Cunliffe

Pictures by Celia Berridge

from the original television designs by Ivor Wood

Cartwheel
·B·O·O·K·S·™

SCHOLASTIC INC.

New York   Toronto   London   Auckland   Sydney

First published by André Deutsch Limited, 1982

ISBN 0-590-47099-X

12 11 10 9 8 7 6 5 4 3 2 1   3 4 5 6 7 8/9

Printed in the U.S.A.   24

First Scholastic Inc. printing, July 1993

One sunny morning, Postman Pat was hurrying along the road with a truckload of letters and parcels for the people of Greendale. Over a hill and around a corner, he had to jam on his brakes because the road was full of sheep.

Pat's cat Jess wanted to know what was going on. He popped his head out of the open window to have a look. Just then, a big ram with great curly horns pushed up to the truck, right in Jess's face! What a fright they both had! Jess jumped down into his basket, and Pat stroked him to cheer him up.

Peter Fogg was driving his sheep across the road with his dogs, Bess and Ben. He opened a gate, and the sheep went into the field, *baaing* and following their leader. Peter waved as he fastened the gate, and Pat went on his way.

But he soon had to stop again — this time for a herd of cows. The cows walked slowly by; they never hurried. Mr. Thompson was walking behind them. He waved his stick and shouted, "Get up, then!" But it made no

difference. The cows *mooed,* stopped to munch the roadside grasses, and took their time. When the road was clear at last, Mr. Thompson waved to Pat, and Pat was on his way again.

When Pat stopped at the village school, he saw Charlie Pringle carrying a bunch of flowers.

"What lovely flowers," said Pat.

"They're for our spring display," said Charlie. "We're all bringing something. Look, here comes Lucy — and Katy and Tom."

They all had something special. Lucy Selby had brought a basket of eggs and Tom Pottage a box of day-old chicks. They all showed Pat what they had brought. Bill Thompson brought a cup of tea for Pat and collected the letters.

Then Pat was off again, away up the steep hills and winding roads. In and out of farmyards he went, delivering cards and letters and parcels. There was an urgent package of medicine for Dr. Forsyth, the vet, and a sweepstakes notice for George Lancaster.

"I wonder if he's won something," said Pat, but George was out in the fields, so he couldn't ask him. It was just about lunchtime and Pat was on the hill above Thompson Ground.

"What a nice place for a picnic," he said. So he parked his truck on the grass by the roadside and Jess jumped out, glad to stretch his legs. Pat locked the truck. They found a sunny place to sit in the field, with a grassy slope to lean against. Several of Mrs. Thompson's hens were scratching about along the hedges.

From this high hill, Pat could see the whole valley, with the Thompsons' farm on the steep hillside just below where he was sitting. Pat thought he could almost peep down the chimney and see Mrs. Thompson putting the kettle on the fire. Jess was thinking about Pat's lunch box and hoping there was a can of sardines in it.

Pat placed the box on the grass, with his keys neatly beside it, so as not to forget them. Then he opened the box. Jess was in luck: there was a whole can of sardines to share with Pat as well as sandwiches, an apple, a yogurt, and a big slice of cherry cake.

They began to eat, but it was so warm in the sun that both Pat and Jess began to feel sleepy. They closed their eyes. Mrs. Thompson's hens were not a bit sleepy. They had spotted Pat's food, too. They pecked their way nearer and nearer to Pat and Jess and the open lunch box.

Then a noise awakened Pat. He sat up and blinked. Two hens were running away with sandwiches in their beaks and a third was pecking at the yogurt. Pat shouted, jumped up, and chased the hens, but he couldn't catch them. Jess chased another into the hedge. Pat ran back to the lunch box just in time to see another bold hen running away with his keys in her beak. He chased her down the hill, but she spread her wings and flew into a tree.

"I must get my keys," said Pat. "I cannot open my truck or deliver my letters without them! Dear me, it's a long time since I climbed a tree, but I'd better try."

Jess stretched his paws up the trunk of the tree, digging his claws in and glaring up at the hen. He could easily climb, but he knew that he couldn't get down again. The bold hen sat on a high branch, with the keys in her beak, looking down at Pat and Jess. Pat began to climb nearer and nearer to the hen.

He was just reaching out to grab the keys, when the hen dropped them into a hollow in the tree and flew off to the farmyard with a loud squawk. Now Pat had to climb higher to search for his keys. He put his foot on a rotten branch. *Crack*! It gave way, and Pat and the branch came tumbling down. Pat landed in the middle of a prickly bush. It broke his fall, but it scratched and prickled him all over.

Mrs. Thompson had heard the commotion and came out to see what was going on. She helped Pat out of the bush and pulled the prickles out of him. He told her all about the thieving hens.

"Dear me," said Mrs. Thompson, "one would think she's a magpie. They're the ones for taking anything shiny. We'd better get a ladder and see if we can find your keys."

"There'll be no mail delivered in the valley unless we do," said Pat.

"That won't do," said Mrs. Thompson, "especially when I'm expecting a letter from Auntie Jean to say if she's coming for Easter."

So they got the ladder and leaned it against the tree. Pat climbed up easily now. While Mrs. Thompson held the ladder, Pat looked among the branches and found the hollow where the hen had dropped his keys. He found a lot of other things there, too.

"It's like a nest," he said. "A magpie's nest."

He brought everything down to show Mrs. Thompson. There were all kinds of shiny things: bits of glass, wire, a bottle cap, buttons, a doll's eye, and something larger among the glittery pieces, as well as Pat's keys.

"That's my wedding ring that's been missing since last Easter. I thought I'd lost it down the sink," cried Mrs. Thompson. "I *am* glad to see it again." She wiped it clean on her dress and put it on her finger.

When they had put the ladder away, she said, "My hens have stolen

your sandwiches, so you'd better come and have some lunch with me —
there's plenty to spare."

Pat was glad he'd lost his sandwiches when he saw what a good lunch
Mrs. Thompson had prepared. So was Jess. He had a tasty plate of fish
and a bowl of creamy milk. It was all much better than even the best of
sandwiches. Mrs. Thompson was happy, too, to see her ring shining on
her finger once more.

It was time to be on their way, and Pat said good-bye and thank you to Mrs. Thompson. As they drove along, Pat's pocket jingled with all the shiny things he had found in the tree.

"Just imagine," he said, "a magpie-hen. Who ever heard of such a thing?"

Jess wondered what a magpie-cat would collect. Farther along the road,

they saw the delivery truck, and Pat stopped to have a chat with Sam Waldron. He told Sam the story of the magpie-hen.

"She'd better keep away from my truck," he said. "I wonder if that's where my tiepin went?"

Pat showed him the hen's collection. But there were no tiepins among the glittery bits.

Pat went on his way. He had some letters for Miss Hubbard and he told her about the magpie-hen.

"Well," she said, "I lost a silver earring last month and a hat pin. I wonder if they're up a tree somewhere?"

Pat showed her the glittery bits.

"That hen could have another hoard in another tree," she said. "I must go and see Mrs. Thompson and have a good look."

Along by Garner Bridge, Pat met George Lancaster on his tractor and stopped to tell *him* about the thieving magpie-hen. George couldn't think of anything he'd lost, but he thought it made a good story.

"Well, but you might have won something," said Pat. "There's a letter for you from the sweepstakes you entered."

"Is there, by Jove? I'll be off then," said George, and he sped away at top speed.

On the way home, Pat saw some real magpies and wondered if they had taught Mrs. Thompson's hens how to steal.

As for Jess, *he* was falling asleep.